The Snail
and the
Whale

by Julia Donaldson

Illustrated by Axel Scheffler

MACMILLAN

This is a tale of a tiny snail

And a great big, grey-blue humpback whale.

This is a rock as black as soot,

And this is a snail with an itchy foot.

The sea snail slithered all over the rock

And gazed at the sea and the ships in the dock.

And as she gazed she sniffed and sighed.

"The sea is deep and the world is wide!

How I long to sail!"

Said the tiny snail.

These are the other snails in the flock,

Who all stuck tight to the smooth black rock

And said to the snail with the itchy foot,

"Be quiet! Don't wriggle! Sit still! Stay put!"

But the tiny sea snail sighed and sniffed,

Then cried, "I've got it! I'll hitch a lift!"

This is the trail

Of the tiny snail,

A silvery trail that looped and curled

And said . . .

This is the whale who came one night

When the tide was high and the stars were bright.

A humpback whale, immensely long,

Who sang to the snail a wonderful song

Of shimmering ice and coral caves

And shooting stars and enormous waves.

And this is the tail

Of the humpback whale.

He held it out of the starlit sea

And said to the snail,

"Come sail with me."

This is the sea,

So wild and free,

That carried the whale

And the snail on his tail

To towering icebergs and far-off lands,

With fiery mountains and golden sands.

These are the waves that arched and crashed,

That foamed and frolicked and sprayed

   and splashed

The tiny snail

On the tail of the whale.

These are the caves

Beneath the waves,

Where stripy fish with feathery fins

And sharks with hideous toothy grins

Swam round the whale

And the snail on his tail.

This is the sky

So vast and high,

Sometimes sunny and blue and warm,

Sometimes filled with a thunderstorm,

With zigzag lightning

Flashing and frightening

The tiny snail

On the tail of the whale.

And she gazed at the sky, the sea, the land,

The waves and the caves and the golden sand,

She gazed and gazed, amazed by it all,

And she said to the whale, "I feel so small."

But then came the day
The whale lost his way . . .

These are the speedboats, running a race,
Zigging and zooming all over the place,
Upsetting the whale with their earsplitting roar,
Making him swim too close to the shore.

This is the tide, slipping away . . .

And this is the whale lying beached
in a bay.

"Quick! Off the sand! Back to sea!"
cried the snail.
"I can't move on land! I'm too big!"
moaned the whale.

The snail felt helpless and terribly small.
Then, "I've got it!" she cried,
and started to crawl.

"I must not fail,"
Said the tiny snail.

This is the bell on the school in the bay,

Ringing the children in from their play.

This is the teacher, holding her chalk,

Telling the class, "Sit straight! Don't talk!"

This is the board, as black as soot . . .

And this is the snail with the itchy foot!

"A snail! A snail!"

The teacher turns pale.

"Look!" say the children.

"It's leaving a trail."

This is the trail

Of the tiny snail,

A silvery trail saying . . .

These are the children, running from school,

Fetching the firemen, digging a pool,

Squirting and spraying to keep the whale cool.

This is the tide coming into the bay,

And these are the villagers shouting, "Hooray!"

As the whale and the snail travel safely away . . .

Back to the dock

And the flock on the rock,

Who said, "How time's flown!"

And, "Haven't you grown!"

And the whale and the snail

Told their wonderful tale

Of shimmering ice and coral caves,

And shooting stars and enormous waves,

And of how the snail, so small and frail,

With her looping, curling, silvery trail,

Saved the life of the humpback whale.

Then the humpback whale

Held out his tail

And on crawled snail after snail after snail.

And they sang to the sea as they all set sail

On the tail of the grey-blue humpback whale.

For everyone at Hillhead Primary School, Wick ~ J.D.

First published 2003 by Macmillan Children's Books
This edition published 2004 by Macmillan Children's Books
a division of Macmillan Publishers Limited
20 New Wharf Road, London N1 9RR
Basingstoke and Oxford
Associated companies throughout the world
www.panmacmillan.com

ISBN: 978-0-333-98224-2

Text copyright © Julia Donaldson 2003
Illustrations copyright © Axel Scheffler 2003
Moral rights asserted

31 33 35 37 36 34 32

A CIP catalogue record for this book is available from the British Library.

Printed in China